Gordon's House

Written and Illustrated
by
Julie Brinckloe

I am going to Gordon's house.
You can go with me
if you want to.
We might make cocoa
and sit by the fire
or walk in the woods
or do almost anything.
Come along, don't be shy.
Gordon is really very nice,
and I know he will like you.

GORDON THE TREE

HOW TO ATTRACT BIRDS

Make believe you are a tree.

Hold some leaves and things...

and don't move.

4

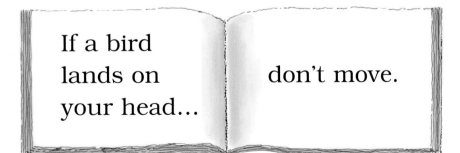

If a bird
lands on
your head...   don't move.

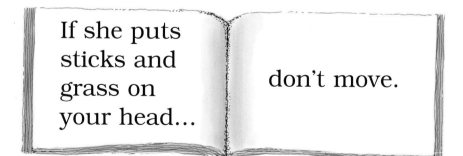

If she puts sticks and grass on your head...

don't move.

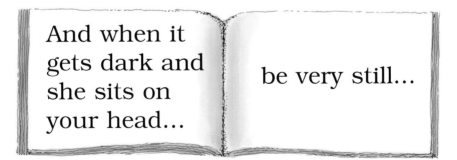

And when it gets dark and she sits on your head...

be very still...

7

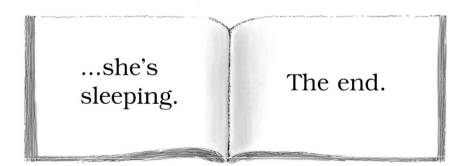

...she's
sleeping.

The end.

 THE BABOON GAME

Gordon and Edith were sitting on a log.

"What shall we do?"
said Edith.

"I don't know," said Gordon.
"Just sit here, I guess."

"No," said Edith. "We'll play a game.

I'll make believe I'm something.
You guess what it is."

Edith thought of a baboon.

She walked back and forth with
her wings drooping.

"Are you a kite with no wind?"
said Gordon.

"No," said Edith. "Guess again."

13

She hopped around and made
grunting sounds.

"Are you a great big rabbit with
a cold?" said Gordon.

"No," said Edith. "Guess again."

She hung from a tree and scratched
her feathers.

"Are you a leaf with fleas?"
said Gordon.
"An apple with worms?
Are you a broken branch with
ants in its pants?"

15

"No, no, no," said Edith.
"I'm a baboon!"

"Oh," said Gordon.
"What's a baboon?"

GORDON AND THE HOPPY THING

Gordon was eating an ice cream cone
when a bug hopped by.

"What are you eating?"
said the bug.

"Ice cream,"
said Gordon.
"Have a lick."

The bug took a lick of ice cream.
It tasted so good that he wanted
the whole cone for himself.

And he thought of a way to get it.

"Hey, there,"
said the bug.
"Can you hop?"

"Yes," said Gordon. "I can hop."

"Can you hop over sticks?"
said the bug.

"Sticks are easy,"
said Gordon.

"Can you hop over stones?" said the bug.

"Yes," said Gordon.
"I can
hop over
stones, too."

"Well, then," said the bug.
"Can you hop
over me?"

"Of course I can," said Gordon.
"You are just a
tiny little bug."

"I'll bet you my cap you can't,"
said the bug.

"I'll bet you my cone I can,"
said Gordon.

20

Gordon tried to hop over the bug.
But the bug was hopping, too.

Gordon hopped
after him.

They hopped over sticks.

They hopped over stones.

They even hopped over a stream.
But Gordon could not hop over
that bug.

"All right, hoppy thing,"
he said finally.
"You win my
ice cream cone."

The bug took Gordon's cone.
He looked inside.
The ice cream was gone!
It had all dripped
out the
bottom.

"My ice cream!" he cried.
"It's all melted away!"

The bug sat on a rock and grumbled,

and Gordon hopped over him
just
like
that.

GORDON
AND THE SCARECROW

Gordon saw a scarecrow in a bean patch.

"Hello," said Gordon.

The scarecrow didn't answer.

Gordon leaned on the garden wall.
"Hey, you. Hello," he said.

The scarecrow didn't answer.

Gordon climbed into the garden.

"Why won't you talk?" he said. "Do you have a cold?"

The scarecrow didn't answer.

"Are you sad?" said Gordon.
"Are you tired of standing in the bean patch all day? Do you want to play with me?"

The scarecrow
didn't answer.

"You don't like me, do you?"
said Gordon.
"You don't want to talk to me.
But I'll *make* you talk."

"I'll pick a bean
from your garden."

Gordon picked the biggest bean he
could find.

"Aren't you going to holler?"
he said to the scarecrow.

The scarecrow
didn't answer.

29

So Gordon ate the bean.

"I ate your bean," he said.
"Hey, scarecrow, I ate your bean."

The scarecrow didn't answer.

Gordon looked at the scarecrow
and scratched his head.

"I don't think you *can* talk," he said.
"You're just an old heap of straw
with no feelings at all."

All at once Gordon felt silly
standing in the
bean patch.

He climbed over the garden wall.

"So long, you old heap of straw,"
he said.

"So long," said the scarecrow.